HIGH SCHOOL MUSICAL 3 SENIOR YEAR

SAY WHAT?

A <u>WILDCATS</u> Fill-In Story
NOUN

HIGH SCHOOL MUSICAL 3 SENIOR YEAR

SAY WHAT?

A <u>WILDCATS</u> Fill-In Story
NOUN

By Avery Scott

Based on the Disney Channel Original Movie
"High School Musical," Written by Peter Barsocchini
Based on "High School Musical 2," Written by Peter Barsocchini
Based on "High School Musical 3: Senior Year," Written by Peter Barsocchini
Based on the screenplay written by Peter Barsocchini
Based on characters created by Peter Barsocchini
Executive Producer Kenny Ortega
Produced by Bill Borden and Barry Rosenbush
Directed by Kenny Ortega

DISNEP PRESS

NEW YORK

INSTRUCTIONS

Need a refresher course on what to say? Here's a list of what's what in the world of grammar!

An adjective helps describe a person or a thing. Some examples are: **smart**, **talented**, **ambitious**, and **studious**.

To explain how something is done, use an adverb. Just a hint: they usually end in -ly. Some examples are: **carefully**, **amazingly**, **wonderfully**, and **impressively**.

A noun is a person, place, or thing. Pretty simple, huh? Some nouns to keep you on track are: **school**, **books**, **homework**, and **laboratory**.

If you want to put some action into the stories, you'll need to use a verb. Some examples are: **believe**, **achieve**, and **compete**. Verbs can also be in past tense, like **aced**, **studied**, and **completed**, or they can end in -ing, like **practicing**, **reading**, and **memorizing**.

What are you waiting for? Put on your thinking cap, grab a pencil, and let's go!

NEW YEAR'S EVE

COME _____ ,
$\qquad$ **NOUN**

COME _____ !
$\qquad$ **PLURAL NOUN**

The Sky Mountain _____ Resort
$\qquad$ **VERB**

invites you to _____ in the New Year!
$\qquad$ **VERB**

Invite all of your _____ and wear
$\qquad$ **PLURAL NOUN**

your fanciest _____ !
$\qquad$ **ARTICLE OF CLOTHING**

Delicious _____ will be served!
$\qquad$ **TYPE OF FOOD (PLURAL)**

Live performances by The _____
$\qquad$ **SILLY WORD**

and _____ !
$\qquad$ **MUSICIAN (FEMALE)**

Plus a/an _____ karaoke contest,
$\qquad$ **ADJECTIVE**

where you could win cool _____ !
$\qquad$ **PLURAL NOUN**

TROY'S TRIP

I love the Sky Mountain Ski Resort. My family and I have been

coming here for over _____ years.
NUMBER

I have been hitting the ski _____ every
PLURAL NOUN

day. I've also been practicing my jump _____
PLURAL NOUN

on the basketball _____. I need to stay on my
PLACE

game, even on vacation! Even though I'd rather spend all my

time _____, my mom is making me
VERB ENDING IN "ING"

go to this New Year's Eve party in the _____ tonight.
PLACE

I guess I'll go check it out. It could be fun!

PARTY PLANS

It's the last night of my ski _____ with my mom.
NOUN

Learning to _____ down those slopes was harder
VERB

than I expected! Oh, guess what? After the New Year, I have

to go to yet another _____ school—back to
ADJECTIVE

reality! Tonight is New Year's Eve, and my mom

_____ wants me to go to the teen
ADVERB

party in the _____. I would much
PLACE

rather read my new _____ and sit by a
NOUN

warm _____!
NOUN

DELIGHTFUL DUET

Little did I know that there would be a karaoke

_____ at the party. Before I knew it, I was pushed

NOUN

onstage and _____ to sing! I knew

VERB (PAST TENSE)

I should've just stayed in and read my _____!

NOUN

I nearly lost my _____ when the spotlight

NOUN

hit me and the music started. I was so nervous I started

to _____. But the _____ boy

VERB **ADJECTIVE**

onstage with me somehow made it all okay.

_____ with him felt so _____. It was

VERB ENDING IN "ING" **ADJECTIVE**

a truly magical _____.

NOUN

SURPRISE PERFORMANCE

When I somehow ended up on the _____ and had
                                    NOUN

to _____, I thought I would _____.
      VERB   VERB

But it turns out that I can really _____! The best
                                        VERB

part, though, was my singing partner. Her name is Gabriella

Montez. After we finished singing our_____, we stepped
                                           NOUN

outside to talk and to look at the bright _____
                                              PLURAL NOUN

in the _____. At the stroke of midnight,
           PLACE

we said _____! But then she had to go back
              SILLY WORD

to her _____ and _____ away.
           PLACE   VERB (PAST TENSE)

KARAOKE 101

Now that Troy and Gabriella have successfully

_____ onstage, here are some _____ for
VERB (PAST TENSE)   PLURAL NOUN

those who also want to be karaoke _____.
                                  OCCUPATION (PLURAL)

1. Pick a _____ that you already know.
          NOUN

2. Choose a song that isn't too _____
                                 ADJECTIVE

   or too _____.
           ADJECTIVE

3. Add a few cool dance _____
                         PLURAL NOUN

   to your routine.

4. After you've finished singing your _____, take a bow!
                                       NOUN

EAST HIGH ROCKS!

Welcome to East High, home of the _____! It's
                                      ANIMAL (PLURAL)

a really great _____ to _____
                   PLACE   VERB

and _____. Our student body is
              VERB

very _____, and all of our _____
        ADJECTIVE   PLURAL NOUN

have lots of school spirit. There are so many fun

extracurricular _____ to join, like the
                    PLURAL NOUN

Drama _____ or the _____. There
          NOUN   SILLY WORD

is even a Scholastic _____, which features
                          NOUN

some of the best and brightest _____ in
                                   PLURAL NOUN

the _____.
       PLACE

FIRST-DAY JITTERS

I am so _____ about my first day
        ADJECTIVE

of school at East High. I couldn't _____ at
                                    VERB

all last night, and it took me _____ hours
                                NUMBER

to pick out the perfect _____ to
                         ARTICLE OF CLOTHING

wear. I cannot believe I'm going to another

_____ school. My mom and I move so
        ADJECTIVE

much! Sometimes I wake up and think I still live in

_____. But at least my mom promised
        PLACE

that I could _____ at East High until
                VERB

graduation— _____!
              EXCLAMATION

THE WILDCATS

The East High basketball _____ is made up
                              NOUN

of the most _____ guys around. They
                ADJECTIVE

can often be seen _____ on the court
                     VERB ENDING IN "ING"

and they always look _____! Troy
                          ADJECTIVE

Bolton is the team's _____, Jason
                          NOUN

Cross plays _____, Chad Danforth
                 NOUN

plays _____, and Zeke
          OCCUPATION

Baylor is the center. Under the leadership of Coach Bolton,

who is also Troy's _____, they are one of the
                        NOUN

top _____ in the _____!
       PLURAL NOUN   PLACE

MORNING ANNOUNCEMENTS

Attention _____ of East High! Tryouts
                    PLURAL NOUN

for the winter _____ are today
                           NOUN

at _____ o'clock. Be sure to bring
          NUMBER

your _____! All students who have not
        PLURAL NOUN

handed in their permission _____ for
                                    PLURAL NOUN

the class trip to _____ must do
                         PLACE

so _____. And don't forget that today
        ADVERB

is the _____ game! Doors open
                ADJECTIVE

at _____ o'clock, and we'll have a live
        NUMBER

performance from the _____ before the
                              SILLY WORD

game. Go _____!
                ANIMAL (PLURAL)

14

SCHOLASTIC DECATHLON

The Scholastic Decathlon Team is probably the most

_____ organization in all of
ADJECTIVE

East High. Our team has _____ members and
NUMBER

has been rated "Most _____" in the entire
ADJECTIVE

_____ for the past _____ years!
PLACE   NUMBER

In each competition, we have to answer questions

about math, science, history, and other school

_____. The team that answers the
PLURAL NOUN

most _____ correctly wins!
PLURAL NOUN

How _____ is that?
ADJECTIVE

PRINCIPAL MATSUI

Principal Matsui is the school _____ of East
                                        NOUN

High. He is _____ and always takes his
              ADJECTIVE

job very _____. He can be really easygoing
            ADVERB

but can also be _____. After all, he does
                  ADJECTIVE

have to look after _____ students! He
                      NUMBER

always has a _____ on his face and loves to
                NOUN

tell _____. You can always count on Principal
        PLURAL NOUN

Matsui when you need a _____! He's a
                          NOUN

really _____ _____!
          ADJECTIVE   OCCUPATION

REUNITED

When I walked into homeroom this morning, I couldn't

believe my _____. I spotted a new
           PLURAL NOUN

_____ that looked a lot like Gabriella
        NOUN

from the ski resort! Luckily I still had her cell phone

_____, and when I dialed the number
        NOUN

I could hear her phone _____, right
                              VERB

there in class! Unfortunately, Ms. Darbus could, too, and

gave us both detention. _____!
                              EXCLAMATION

But who cares about detention; I can't believe the girl of my

_____ is right here at East High!
   PLURAL NOUN

QUEEN BEE

Hello, East High! If you don't already know me, my name

is Sharpay Evans. I am a member of the Drama _____,
NOUN

and I always star in our _____. I love
PLURAL NOUN

to wear fashionable _____,
ARTICLE OF CLOTHING (PLURAL)

especially if they are _____. I have a
COLOR

twin brother named Ryan, who is really _____
ADJECTIVE

and helps me carry my _____! It's not easy
PLURAL NOUN

being the most popular _____ in school.
NOUN

ALL ABOUT RYAN

I'm sure you've already met my _____ sister,
ADJECTIVE

Sharpay. I'm Ryan Evans, her twin _____.
NOUN

We have a lot of the same _____, like
PLURAL NOUN

singing and _____. We both love
VERB ENDING IN "ING"

spending our summers at the _____.
PLACE

And we _____ share a passion for fashion!
ADVERB

I have more pairs of _____ than
PLURAL NOUN

she does! But overall, I guess I'm a little quieter and

less _____ than my sister. We
ADJECTIVE

can't both be the _____ of the
PLURAL NOUN

family!

BEST FRIENDS

Troy and I have been best buds since we were both little _____ PLURAL NOUN. He is the most _____ ADJECTIVE guy around. Not only is he great at _____ VERB ENDING IN "ING" basketball, but he's also a really good _____ NOUN. He has always been there for me when I've needed him.

Sometimes I can act really _____ ADJECTIVE, especially if we lose a basketball _____ NOUN. But Troy always knows exactly what to _____ VERB to _____ VERB me down. We're not just best friends — we're more like _____ PLURAL NOUN!

CHANCE ENCOUNTER

I cannot believe that Troy Bolton _____ goes to
ADVERB

school here! It's like a _____ come true. When he waited
NOUN

for me after class and said _____, I thought
SILLY WORD

I might _____. We talked for _____ minutes,
VERB   *NUMBER*

and then he told me about the auditions for the next

winter _____. I'm way too _____ to
NOUN   *ADJECTIVE*

do that! But if we could sing together again someday,

I'd be the happiest _____ at East High!
NOUN

Gabriella

RUNNING THE SHOW

When I saw Troy talking to the new girl, Gabriella, I

almost _____. *Hel-lo?* Doesn't she know
VERB (PAST TENSE)

that I am the most _____ girl at school? And
ADJECTIVE

to think that they were _____ right in
VERB ENDING IN "ING"

front of the sign-up sheet for the winter _____.
NOUN

_____! She *obviously* doesn't
EXCLAMATION

know how things work around here. I told her that Ryan and

I always star as the lead _____ in all of the
PLURAL NOUN

musicals. She shouldn't even waste her _____ and
NOUN

try to _____ with me!
VERB

SOMETHING NEW

At basketball practice today, I asked Chad if he thought I

should _____ for the winter musical.
                    VERB

I think it would be so much fun. I'd get the chance to

_____ with _____! Plus, it would
      VERB   CELEBRITY (FEMALE)

look really good on my college _____. Hey, I
                                      PLURAL NOUN

might even get into my dream school, _____!
                                              PLACE

But Chad didn't really agree. He said that musicals are

kind of _____.
              ADJECTIVE

KEEP YOUR HEAD IN THE GAME

I couldn't stop _____ all during
VERB ENDING IN "ING"

basketball practice. But I need to _____ and
VERB

keep my head in the _____! The Wildcats
NOUN

just *have* to _____ the championship this year.
VERB

We've been _____ so hard! But every time
VERB ENDING IN "ING"

I go to _____ the ball, I
VERB

think about how cool it was when Gabriella and I

were _____ onstage
VERB ENDING IN "ING"

at the _____. It was one of the best
PLACE

_____ of my life!
PLURAL NOUN

WHO'S THAT GIRL?

Today's chemistry class was full of _____.

 **PLURAL NOUN**

The new _____ , Gabriella, is so _____!

 **NOUN** **ADJECTIVE**

She totally knew that our teacher _____ made

 **CELEBRITY (FEMALE)**

a mistake and she actually corrected her! I'm usually the

only _____ who does that. I think Gabriella is

 **NOUN**

totally going to be my new best _____.

 **SILLY WORD**

And I'm *definitely* asking her if she wants to join the

Scholastic _____.

 **NOUN**

25

RYAN'S DISCOVERY

Today I saw the strangest _____. Troy

NOUN

Bolton was _____ near the

VERB ENDING IN "ING"

winter musical audition sign-up _____.

NOUN

When I told Sharpay, she started to _____ and

VERB

_____. I didn't know what to do! I mean, I knew

VERB

she would be upset, but I never expected her to start

_____ like that! But then she told me that

VERB ENDING IN "ING"

she saw Troy and _____ hanging

PERSON IN THE ROOM (FEMALE)

out by the sign-in _____ earlier that day, too.

NOUN

THE INSIDE SCOOP

I decided to find out once and for all what this new girl

Gabrielle Montez is really about. Ryan and I went

to the _____ to see if we could find any

             PLACE

_____ about her online. And guess what? It

      NOUN

turns out she is some sort of whiz _____!

                                          NOUN

There were all these _____ that said

                     PLURAL NOUN

Gabriella is one smart _____. She's won,

                 TYPE OF FOOD

like, over _____ academic awards. Now I can

         NUMBER

finally _____ a sigh of relief. She'd never

       VERB

have time to _____ for the winter musical!

         VERB

27

SAME OLD SITUATION

After detention was over, Taylor and I went for a

_____. She explained the way things _____
   NOUN   **VERB**

at East High. Guys like Troy Bolton and his friend

_____ play _____ and
CELEBRITY (MALE)   **TYPE OF SPORT**

hang out with the cheerleaders and _____.
                                    PLURAL NOUN

And _____ like me and Taylor, well, we
    PLURAL NOUN

always _____ together after school in the
       VERB

_____ and study so we can get
PLACE

straight _____ and get into a
         PLURAL NOUN

good _____ when we _____. I guess
     NOUN   **VERB**

East High is just like all the other _____ I've
                                     PLURAL NOUN

been to.

DETENTION ALREADY?

I can't believe I got detention on my very first

day at _____! I tried to do
_{PLACE}

my _____ homework, but I couldn't
_{SCHOOL SUBJECT}

stop _____ over at Troy. Every
_{VERB ENDING IN "ING"}

time I looked at him, my face would turn bright

_____. But guess what? I made a
_{COLOR}

new friend! Taylor McKessie, the girl from my chemistry

_____, asked me to join the Scholastic
_{NOUN}

Decathlon team—where _____ get to
_{PLURAL NOUN}

compete against other _____!
_{PLURAL NOUN}

Gabriella

AUDITIONING 101

As a drama teacher, I take my _____ *very* seriously. If
NOUN

you are planning to _____ for the winter musical,
VERB

please keep the following suggestions in mind.

Be on time! The theater is a very serious _____
NOUN

and not a moment should be wasted.

Always be sure to wear your best _____
ARTICLE OF CLOTHING

and brush your _____.
NOUN

Make sure to _____ a song that you know
VERB

the _____ to.
PLURAL NOUN

When you have finished _____, take
VERB ENDING IN "ING"

a deep _____ and _____!
NOUN   VERB

SNEAKING AROUND

Even though I should really stick to playing _____,
TYPE OF SPORT

I decided that I would _____ for the winter
VERB

musical. But I had to be really careful not to let

anyone _____ me, especially my dad. All
VERB

he wants is for me to practice my jump _____ on
PLURAL NOUN

the basketball _____. I had to hide behind
NOUN

a _____, run through the _____, and
NOUN   PLACE

then I was finally able to _____ backstage.
VERB

I grabbed a _____ and used it to hide behind
NOUN

as I _____ down the ramp. Whew!
VERB (PAST TENSE)

Just then, I felt a tap on my _____! To my
NOUN

surprise, Gabriella was there for the audition, too!

31

KELSI THE COMPOSER

I was so excited when Ms. Darbus picked me to be the

_____ of this year's winter musical! There's
OCCUPATION

nothing I like more than _____ at
VERB ENDING IN "ING"

a piano, writing _____. I am
PLURAL NOUN

so _____ that my music has been chosen
ADJECTIVE

for _____! I've written over _____ pieces,
SILLY WORD   NUMBER

and I can't wait for _____ to hear them. I've
CELEBRITY (FEMALE)

been _____ my whole _____ for
VERB ENDING IN "ING"   NOUN

this opportunity. It's so _____. I just hope
ADJECTIVE

that _____ likes them. After all, she
PERSON IN ROOM (FEMALE)

is always the lead _____!
NOUN

Kelsi

AMAZING AUDITION

Ryan and I were the only _____ that
PLURAL NOUN

_____ for the lead in
VERB (PAST TENSE)

Twinkle _____. After all, we *are*
SILLY WORD

the _____ of the school! Kelsi Nielsen thought
PLURAL NOUN

that she was going to _____ the song that she wrote
VERB

on the _____, but we decided to redo her song
NOUN

and played it on our_____ instead.
NOUN

We wore bright _____ and
ARTICLE OF CLOTHING (PLURAL)

_____ our _____ out.
VERB (PAST TENSE)   PLURAL NOUN

When the song ended, we both took a deep

_____, and everyone applauded and
NOUN

yelled _____!
EXCLAMATION

33

SPEAKING UP

As I watched the auditions, I felt like I had a _____
NUMBER

_____ in my stomach.
TYPE OF ANIMAL (PLURAL)

I really wanted to _____, but I was so nervous! Just
VERB

as Ms. Darbus _____ that the auditions
VERB (PAST TENSE)

were over, I yelled _____! To my
EXCLAMATION

surprise, Troy shouted _____ and told Ms. Darbus
SILLY WORD

he wanted to try out, too! But Ms. Darbus wouldn't let us

_____ because we were _____ minutes
VERB   NUMBER

late. I was so _____ I almost started
ADJECTIVE

to _____.
VERB

Gabriella

34

A SURPRISE CALLBACK

Gabriella and I were really _____ that
ADJECTIVE

Ms. Darbus wouldn't let us _____. As
VERB

we were about to _____ out
VERB (PAST TENSE)

of the auditorium, I noticed that Kelsi had dropped all of

her _____, so I stopped to _____ her. I
PLURAL NOUN   VERB

asked her if she could play something that Gabriella

and I could _____ together. When we
VERB

started _____, our voices
VERB ENDING IN "ING"

were in perfect _____. To our surprise,
NOUN

Ms. Darbus had been _____ the whole time, and
VERB ENDING IN "ING"

she told us that we had gotten a callback for the audition!

35

ROLE REVERSALS

What on _____ is going on around
PLACE

here? The callbacks for the winter musical are posted, and

I am not _____ about it! Of
ADJECTIVE

course, my name and Ryan's are there, but so are Troy's

and Gabriella's! When did they even _____?
VERB

I cannot _believe_ this is _____ happening.
ADVERB

Ryan thinks that maybe it is a joke and that we are

being filmed for the show _____,and
SILLY WORD

_____ is going to jump out at any
CELEBRITY (MALE)

second and yell _____. I hope
EXCLAMATION

that's the case!

CAFETERIA CHAOS

Today in the cafeteria, everyone was acting really

_____. News spread _____ that Troy
   ADJECTIVE   ADVERB

and Gabriella auditioned for *Twinkle* _____,
                                              SILLY WORD

and I guess kids didn't expect it from a jock and a

_____ like Gabriella. So a bunch of _____
   NOUN   PLURAL NOUN

started _____ what they really like to
        VERB ENDING IN "ING"

do. Martha Cox, one of the _____ kids, jumped
                                ADJECTIVE

up and shouted "_____! Hip-hop is my passion!"
                    SILLY WORD

I decided to let everyone in on my secret—that I love to bake

_____ and _____.
TYPE OF FOOD (PLURAL)   PLURAL NOUN

BACK TO BASICS

_____, I don't know what's going on in school
SILLY WORD

today! I decided to have a heart to _____ with
NOUN

Troy and tell him that this _____ he
VERB ENDING IN "ING"

has of starring in the school _____ is crazy.
NOUN

I mean, he's the _____ of the Wildcats! He
NOUN

needs to _____. Who's going to
VERB

practice _____ jump shots with me
VERB ENDING IN "ING"

on the court? What's next? Will Jason Cross admit that

he'd really rather be _____ in
VERB ENDING IN "ING"

the _____ than shooting hoops?
PLACE

MARTHA'S NEW FRIEND

I am so excited that Gabriella is a _____ here

NOUN

at East High! She's in all of my Advanced Placement

_____, and she is really _____.

PLURAL NOUN   ADJECTIVE

She is always the first _____ to raise her hand,

NOUN

and she _____ has all the right answers.

ADVERB

Gabriella's my _____ partner, and together

VERB

we are a _____ to be reckoned with. There's

NOUN

not an equation or _____ that we can't

NOUN

figure out!

Martha

HOOP DREAMS

I love being a _____ of
NOUN

the Wildcats! There's nothing that I would rather do than

practice my _____. The other guys
PLURAL NOUN

on the team are really _____, and
ADJECTIVE

we always have a good _____ together.
NOUN

I've been _____ basketball since I was
VERB ENDING IN "ING"

just a little _____ . One day I want to go to
NOUN

_____ and play for the _____.
PLACE   FAMOUS SPORTS TEAM

How _____ would that be?
ADJECTIVE

TAYLOR'S STUDY TIPS

Follow my _____, and you'll be getting
         PLURAL NOUN

straight _____ in no time!
         PLURAL NOUN

1. Always _____ in a well-lit room, so your
              VERB

_____ don't get tired.
PLURAL NOUN

2. Study somewhere _____, where no one
                        ADJECTIVE

will _____ you.
     VERB

3. _____ a chapter each night so you'll be well prepared
   VERB

the next time your teacher gives a pop _____.
                                          NOUN

4. On the day of a big test, remember to gets lots of

_____ the night before and eat a good breakfast,
NOUN

like scrambled _____.
                PLURAL NOUN

Taylor

41

COACH BOLTON

I love being the _____ of the Wildcats! It's
                        NOUN

really _____. Every day after school
              ADJECTIVE

my team gathers in the _____ and we do
                              PLACE

push-ups and _____ as a warm-up. I make
                    PLURAL NOUN

them run around the gym _____ times,
                                NUMBER

and then we finally get to _____ hoops.
                                  VERB

It makes me so _____ that my
                        ADJECTIVE

son, Troy, is the _____ of the Wildcats. He
                        NOUN

is so _____— I just know he's
              ADJECTIVE

going to be the _____ of the
                        OCCUPATION

_____ someday!
FAMOUS SPORTS TEAM

SECRETS REVEALED

Since I already told practically the whole _____ that
PLACE

my secret hobby is baking, I decided to tell Sharpay

how I really _____ about her. I might as well
VERB

reveal all of my _____ today, right? But when I
PLURAL NOUN

tried to _____ to her, she just _____.
VERB   **VERB (PAST TENSE)**

I tried to act _____ and asked her to
ADJECTIVE

watch me play _____, but she just
TYPE OF SPORT

said _____ and rolled her
SILLY WORD

_____. I even offered to bake her
PLURAL NOUN

_____, but then she
TYPE OF FOOD (PLURAL)

_____away.
VERB (PAST TENSE)

SURPRISE NEWS

I was _____ in my _____ eating
     VERB ENDING IN "ING"   PLACE

a delicious _____ when who _____
             TYPE OF FOOD   VERB ENDING IN "S"

but Ms. Darbus! I was so shocked I almost yelled

_____. When she told me that
     SILLY WORD

Troy had auditioned for her musical, I almost

_____ on my _____.
  VERB (PAST TENSE)   SAME TYPE OF FOOD

My son, a/an _____? Luckily
             OCCUPATION

Ms. Darbus knew from my reaction that it must've just been

a/an _____ joke. After all, Troy is
        ADJECTIVE

way too busy playing _____ to
            TYPE OF SPORT

sing in some school _____.
         NOUN

Coach Bolton

44

LOCKER SURPRISE

When I found a _____ in my locker from Troy,
NOUN

I almost shouted _____! He told
EXCLAMATION

me to meet him in the secret garden on the

_____. I _____ up
PLACE   VERB (PAST TENSE)

the stairs and found him _____ on
VERB ENDING IN "ING"

a bench. We talked for _____ minutes, and
NUMBER

he told me he wanted to do the callbacks for the musical!

Imagine, me and Troy onstage again. It's like a

_____ come true!
NOUN

PRACTICE MAKES PERFECT

Troy and I have been _____ like crazy.

VERB ENDING IN "ING"

We want to be really prepared for the callbacks! But

since we decided not to tell _____,

PERSON IN THE ROOM (MALE)

we have to be really careful that no one _____

VERB ENDING IN "S"

us. I _____ all of my songs in

VERB

the _____, while Troy

TYPE OF ROOM

has to sing in the _____. Isn't

PLACE

that _____? Hopefully, all of

ADJECTIVE

our _____ work will pay off!

ADJECTIVE

Gabriella

DETENTION, AGAIN?

When I found out that Troy had detention with Ms. Darbus

again, I almost _____! I mean, that

                                         VERB (PAST TENSE)

was _____ times in one week. Doesn't

               NUMBER

she know that the team _____ are coming

                         PLURAL NOUN

up? We have to _____ all we can!

                     VERB

Troy seems so _____ lately. Ever

                     ADJECTIVE

since _____ started at East

             CELEBRITY (FEMALE)

High, his _____ has been elsewhere.

                 NOUN

Does he really think he's going to _____ in

                                     VERB

Twinkle Towne? _____!

                         EXCLAMATION

Coach Bolton

47

LIBRARY CONFERENCE

Today was really _____. Chad and I
                         ADJECTIVE

were _____ in the library
        VERB ENDING IN "ING"

when he started telling me that I've been slacking on my

basketball _____. He said that the rest
                 NOUN

of the _____ might lose their
        TYPE OF ANIMAL (PLURAL)

focus if I am too busy _____
                          VERB ENDING IN "ING"

onstage than _____ on the
                VERB ENDING IN "ING"

court. I guess I _____ thought I
                    ADVERB

could do both, but maybe Chad is right. After all, he is my

best _____.
        NOUN

CHAD'S PLAN

Since I am Troy's best _____, I decided
            NOUN

it was time to put a plan into action. I grabbed Jason and

Zeke, and we _____ to the chemistry
        VERB (PAST TENSE)

_____ to _____ to Taylor. At first
      NOUN   **VERB**

she was _____, but then she agreed with
        ADJECTIVE

everything we were _____. I mean, she
            VERB ENDING IN "ING"

wanted Gabriella to focus on the Scholastic Decathlon team,

and we wanted our team _____ back. It made
                NOUN

perfect _____!
      NOUN

SHARPAY'S SURPRISE

Little did Chad and the rest of the _____ know

NOUN

that Ryan and I just *happened* to be _____

VERB ENDING IN "ING"

past the chemistry _____ when we heard them

NOUN

talking about Troy and Gabriella. We couldn't hear exactly

what they were _____, but I bet it

VERB ENDING IN "ING"

has to be something about _____ *Towne*!

SILLY WORD

If Ryan and I don't get to star as the leads, then I will

simply _____. For the sake of the Drama Club and

VERB

all of my fellow actors and _____, the

OCCUPTION (PLURAL)

show must *only* feature the _____ stars

ADJECTIVE

of East High!

PLAN OF ACTION

The next day in the _____, we decided to

PLACE

put our plan into action. As soon as Troy walked in, I showed

him a bunch of _____ that the Wildcats

PLURAL NOUN

have won over the years. Zeke showed him some photos

of _____ to remind him to keep

FAMOUS ATHLETE (MALE)

his _____ in the game. I got the rest of the

NOUN

team to chant _____ while I explained to

SILLY WORD

Troy that the team has to keep their _____ on

PLURAL NOUN

the prize. After all, the championship _____ is

NOUN

only _____ days away!

NUMBER

TAYLOR'S TASK

While Chad and the rest of the _____ were
PLURAL NOUN

trying to convince Troy to focus on the

championship _____ coming up, the rest of
NOUN

the Scholastic Decathlon _____ and I gathered in
PLURAL NOUN

the _____ and talked to Gabriella about
PLACE

_____. We showed her_____of
SCHOOL SUBJECT   **PLURAL NOUN**

famous politicians like _____ and
CELEBRITY (MALE)

_____, hoping she would decide
PERSON IN THE ROOM (FEMALE)

to _____ the Scholastic _____ team
VERB   **SILLY WORD**

instead of singing with _____.
PERSON IN THE ROOM (MALE)

LIVE FROM THE LOCKER ROOM

I was just about to tell Taylor that I had to go meet Kelsi in

the _____ to practice singing, when
         PLACE

all of sudden I heard a loud _____. It was
                                  NOUN

Troy's voice coming through the _____ in
                                 PLURAL NOUN

the chemistry lab. _____! We could all
                      EXCLAMATION

hear Troy talking to the _____ and telling the
                          SILLY WORD

Wildcats that I was just some _____ and that he'd really
                                NOUN

rather _____ than hang out with me. I couldn't
        VERB

believe my _____. I was
            PLURAL NOUN

so _____.
      ADJECTIVE

Gabriella

WHAT'S HAPPENING?

Gabriella is acting so _____. When I tried

to _____ **VERB** to her at her locker, she looked at

me _____ **ADVERB** and started to _____ **VERB**.

Then she told me she didn't want to go to the callbacks for

the musical! She told me she is now an official member of

the _____ **SILLY WORD** so she'll need to _____ **VERB**,

and that I should focus on the big _____ **NOUN** that's

coming up. _____ **EXCLAMATION**! I can't believe it. I don't

want to sing onstage with anyone else.

THE CALLBACKS ARE COMING!

I can't believe that the callbacks for the _____
                                          NOUN

are only _____ days away. There are
        NUMBER

so many things that I still have to _____.
                                   VERB

I need to practice _____, buy some
                  VERB ENDING IN "ING"

new _____, and make sure that
   ARTICLE OF CLOTHING (PLURAL)

I know the lyrics to all of Kelsi's _____.
                                   PLURAL NOUN

I should probably make sure to _____ my
                               VERB

hair, too. Oh, and I think I'll call _____ to
                                    PERSON IN ROOM (FEMALE)

see if she has any _____ advice before
                   ADJECTIVE

the big day!

THEATER RULES

1. Make sure to always wear lots of _____
   PLURAL NOUN

   on your _____, so the audience can really
   NOUN

   see you.

2. Never look directly into the bright _____.
   PLURAL NOUN

   You won't be able to _____!
   VERB

3. Before a fellow actor goes onstage, tell them to

   break a _____. It's good luck!
   NOUN

4. When the audience starts _____
   VERB ENDING IN "ING"

   at the end of the performance, take a deep _____
   NOUN

   and _____!
   VERB

A SURPRISE VISITOR

Tonight, Troy came to _____ to see me. I
PLACE

told _____ not to let him in, so
PERSON IN ROOM (FEMALE)

he _____ all the way up the balcony! I
VERB (PAST TENSE)

felt like I was in a scene from _____. He said
MOVIE

he felt really _____, and that he had made a
ADJECTIVE

big _____. I was so _____
NOUN   ADJECTIVE

I wanted to yell _____!
SILLY WORD

TOGETHER AGAIN

_____! You should have heard Troy and Gabriella
EXCLAMATION

_____ in the _____ today.
VERB ENDING IN "ING"   PLACE

Their _____ were totally in sync and they
PLURAL NOUN

sounded really _____. I think they have
ADJECTIVE

a good chance at starring as the lead _____.
PLURAL NOUN

My sister, _____, is *not*
CELEBRITY (FEMALE)

going to be happy when she hears about this. I hope she

doesn't _____!
VERB

A REVISED PLAN

I simply could *not* let _____ and

CELEBRITY (MALE)

_____ _____ at

PERSON IN ROOM (FEMALE)   VERB

the callbacks. As _____ of the Drama Club,

OCCUPATION

I need to do what is best for the production. And that means

that I always get to star as the lead _____! So,

NOUN

I spoke with Ms. Darbus and convinced her to change the day

of the audition to _____ instead.

DAY OF THE WEEK

Luckily, she agreed. I hope my_____ works!

NOUN

WILDCATS UNITE

When Gabriella and I found that the day of the

_____ was changed, we were shocked. We have
    PLURAL NOUN

been _____ so hard for this! Kelsi
      VERB ENDING IN "ING"

told us that it was all Sharpay's _____.
                                 NOUN

But we're not going to let Sharpay, or anyone else, stop us!

Luckily, the _____ of the Scholastic
            PLURAL NOUN

Decathlon and the Wildcats agreed to work together as a

_____ so we could _____ at the callbacks.
  NOUN   **VERB**

THE BIG DAY

Today is a really _____ day here at
ADJECTIVE

East High! It's the day of the callbacks for the _____,
NOUN

the Wildcats are playing against the _____,
PROFESSIONAL SPORTS TEAM

and my team, the Scholastic Decathlon, is going to compete

against _____! And
CELEBRITY (FEMALE)

guess what? The Wildcats surprised us and gave us a huge

_____ to wish us luck. We had
TYPE OF FOOD

a surprise for them, too—we decorated a huge banner that

read Go _____. And Chad was wearing a
SILLY WORD

T-shirt that read Go, Drama _____!
NOUN

61

FIERCE COMPETITION

I am so _____ that our
ADJECTIVE

team won the first part of the competition of the Scholastic

Decathlon! I knew Gabriella could _____ it!
VERB

She finished writing the answer to the _____ just
NOUN

seconds before _____ did. I was so
CELEBRITY (MALE)

excited, I yelled _____! Everyone
EXCLAMATION

started _____ and _____.
VERB ENDING IN "ING"   VERB ENDING IN "ING"

It was really awesome!

OPERATION CALLBACKS, PHASE I

As soon as the _____ rang and the basketball
_____ NOUN _____

game began, everyone started _____. It
_____ VERB ENDING IN "ING" _____

was so _____. I _____ the
_____ ADJECTIVE _____ _____ VERB (PAST TENSE) _____

ball to _____, and he started
_____ CELEBRITY (MALE) _____

to _____. But the game didn't last long
_____ VERB _____

because suddenly the _____ started
_____ PLURAL NOUN _____

blinking and the lights started to _____!
_____ VERB _____

Principal Matsui announced that everyone had to

leave the _____ in an orderly fashion. Now
_____ PLACE _____

Troy will get to _____ for the musical!
_____ VERB _____

I'm so glad I had a change of heart—Troy's going to

totally _____ the audition!
_____ VERB _____

CHAD

I knew Chad's _____ would work! Now
                        NOUN

I have to put my plan into action. Just as the

experiment part of the Scholastic Decathlon was about

to _____, I _____ on my computer
   VERB   **VERB (PAST TENSE)**

and waited _____ to see what would happen
                  ADVERB

next. Just then, a beaker full of _____
                                    TYPE OF LIQUID

started to _____! _____ yelled
              VERB   **PERSON IN ROOM (MALE)**

_____, and we all had to leave the room. I told
  EXCLAMATION

Gabriella to _____ to the _____ so she could
                VERB   **PLACE**

make the callbacks for the _____.
                                NOUN

A SURPRISE PERFORMANCE

I cannot believe it! Troy and _____ actually
<u>PERSON IN ROOM (FEMALE)</u>

_____ to the callbacks! So much for my
<u>VERB (PAST TENSE)</u>

_____ plan! And then _____ showed
<u>ADJECTIVE</u>   <u>CELEBRITY (FEMALE)</u>

up and offered to play the _____. But
<u>NOUN</u>

when they started to _____, I stood there in
<u>VERB</u>

shock. They sounded so _____. Troy was looking
<u>ADJECTIVE</u>

into Gabriella's _____ and _____,
<u>PLURAL NOUN</u>   <u>VERB ENDING IN "ING"</u>

and Gabriella's voice sounded really _____. When
<u>ADJECTIVE</u>

they finished their _____, I almost _____ but
<u>NOUN</u>   <u>VERB (PAST TENSE)</u>

then caught myself. They *are* the competition, after all!

Sharpay

65

A MAGICAL MOMENT

When Troy and I started _____ together,
VERB ENDING IN "ING"

it was so _____. At first I was
ADJECTIVE

really _____, but I just looked over
ADJECTIVE

at Troy and started to _____. Our voices
VERB

blended together _____, and we sounded
ADVERB

really _____. We _____ together
ADJECTIVE   VERB (PAST TENSE)

and pretended we were the only _____ in
PLURAL NOUN

the room. When we finished _____, everyone
VERB ENDING IN "ING"

started _____ and yelled _____!
VERB ENDING IN "ING"   SILLY WORD

BACK TO THE GAME

After Gabriella and I finished _____, it was time

VERB ENDING IN "ING"

to resume the basketball _____. When we got

NOUN

back on the _____, the competition

PLACE

was _____. It was the last few _____ of

ADJECTIVE   PLURAL NOUN

the game, and the Wildcats were behind. I was

determined for our team to _____. I

VERB

_____ across the court and threw

VERB (PAST TENSE)

the _____ and made the shot! Just then the

NOUN

buzzer _____, and we won! The crowd

VERB (PAST TENSE)

started _____, and everyone

VERB ENDING IN "ING"

was really _____.

ADJECTIVE

A GRAND FINALE

When Troy and I finished _____, it was time to

head   back   to   the   Scholastic   Decathlon   to   finish

the _____. And guess what? We _____!

  NOUN   VERB (PAST TENSE)

    VERB ENDING IN "ING"

Taylor and I were so _____ we yelled _____!

                        ADJECTIVE   SILLY WORD

Everyone in the audience started to _____.

                                                    VERB

I'm so glad Taylor asked me to be a member of the

_____. I really like it here at East High. Today

        NOUN

showed me that no matter what type of _____ you

                                                          NOUN

are, you can be anything you want to be.

EAST HIGH YEARBOOK

Now that it's the end of the school _____, the annual
                                         NOUN

East High Yearbook has been distributed. Check out

this _____ list!
         ADJECTIVE

Most Likely to Succeed: _____
                                    PERSON IN ROOM (FEMALE)

_____ Dressed: _____
        ADJECTIVE   **CELEBRITY (MALE)**

Most Likely to Become a/an _____: Taylor
                                       OCCUPATION

Cutest _____: _____
            NOUN   **YOUR FAVORITE *HIGH SCHOOL MUSICAL* CHARACTER**

Most _____: Chad
              ADJECTIVE

Nicest _____: Sharpay
                PLURAL NOUN

Life of the _____: _____
                      NOUN   **YOUR NAME**

WORKING FOR THE SUMMER

Now that summer is _____ here, I decided to look
                        ADVERB

for a _____ so I could save some extra _____.
        NOUN   NOUN

And guess what? I got a call from Mr.Fulton today! He is the

_____ at the Lava Springs _____ Club,
OCCUPATION   SILLY WORD

and he offered me a _____. I also mentioned that
                        NOUN

Gabriella and a bunch of other _____ from
                                  PLURAL NOUN

East High were looking for jobs, too. We're all going to get

to _____ together this summer.
        VERB

_____!
EXCLAMATION

THE GANG'S ALL HERE!

I can't believe Troy helped me get a job at the _____.
PLACE

I'm going to be a/an _____, which is really cool.
OCCUPATION

Zeke and Martha are going to _____ in the kitchen,
VERB

Chad and Troy will be _____ as
VERB ENDING IN "ING"

_____, Taylor will be the
OCCUPATION (PLURAL)

_____, and Kelsi will be playing
NOUN

the _____ in the _____.
NOUN   PLACE

We're going to have so much fun this summer!

SHARPAY'S PLAN

I can't believe my _____ to have Troy work at
NOUN

Lava Springs is ruined! I mean, yeah, he gets to _____
VERB

here, but so do the other _____!
TYPE OF ANIMAL (PLURAL)

That's *not* what I had in mind. I thought it would just

be Troy and me, _____ in the pool
VERB ENDING IN "ING"

and _____ on the tennis courts.
VERB ENDING IN "ING"

I am so mad that I want to _____!
VERB

SPLISH, SPLASH!

After Gabriella and I finished _____ today,
                                     VERB ENDING IN "ING"

we snuck into the pool to go for a _____.
                                            NOUN

The water was so _____! We played
                           ADJECTIVE

Marco _____ and took turns splashing each
            SILLY WORD

other with _____. We were having so
                  TYPE OF LIQUID

much fun, until our boss _____ caught
                                  CELEBRITY (MALE)

us and told us to _____ home. So much
                          VERB

for a late-night swim!

MR. FULTON

I am Mr. Fulton, the _____ at the Lava
OCCUPATION

_____ Country Club in _____.
PLURAL NOUN   PLACE

It's the finest facility in all of the _____!
                                        COUNTRY

This summer, we have hired many East High students

to _____ for us here at the club. But
     VERB

_____ has requested that I be
CELEBRITY (FEMALE)

a little harder on them. So, I told them that I require that they

_____ at _____ o'clock and that
VERB   NUMBER

their lunch breaks be no longer than _____ minutes.
                                        NUMBER

Otherwise, they're fired!

SUMMER TALENT SHOW

The talent show at the _____ is going to
PLACE

be so _____. I'm going to
ADJECTIVE

wear my favorite _____ and put my hair in
ARTICLE OF CLOTHING

_____, just like _____ does. I'm
PLURAL NOUN   PERSON IN ROOM (FEMALE)

sure that I'll be able to convince Troy to _____ with
VERB

me. The only thing that I still have to decide are which songs

we're going to _____ together.
VERB

ONCE UPON A SONG

I am composing a/an _____ new
ADJECTIVE

song for the talent show at the country club. I wrote

the song especially for _____ and
PERSON IN ROOM (MALE)

_____. I hope they'll agree to
CELEBRITY (FEMALE)

_____ it! They inspire the music in me!
VERB

I also want all the other _____ to
TYPE OF ANIMAL (PLURAL)

do the backup _____ and
VERB ENDING IN "ING"

to _____ around the stage. That would
VERB

be really _____!
ADJECTIVE

Kelsi

BIG PROMOTION

Today, Mr. Fulton promoted me! I am going to be a/an

_____ on the golf course. I get a
OCCUPATION

huge _____, I don't have to _____
NOUN   VERB

in each morning and night, and I'm getting paid

_____ dollars a week. _____!
NUMBER   SILLY WORD

I was also given _____ clothes
ADJECTIVE

and leather shoes imported from _____. I have
COUNTRY

a locker, a new set of _____ to play golf
PLURAL NOUN

with, and even my own golf cart with a _____ on
NUMBER

its hood.

STAR DAZZLE TALENT SHOW

The _____ Annual
           PLACE

Star Dazzle Talent Show

When: _____ p.m. on July _____
          NUMBER   **NUMBER**

Where: _____
                PLACE

_____ and _____
PLURAL NOUN   **TYPE OF FOOD (PLURAL)**

will be served.

Make your _____ now,
              PLURAL NOUN

before the _____ is sold out!
               NOUN

MIXED FEELINGS

Ever since Troy got his new job as a/an _____,
OCCUPATION

we haven't been able to spend much time together.

I really _____ him. I think the other
VERB

_____ are starting to feel the same way, too.
PLURAL NOUN

It's great that he's hanging out with _____
CELEBRITY (MALE)

and playing _____ with _____,
TYPE OF SPORT   PERSON IN ROOM (FEMALE)

but what about us? Doesn't he miss _____
VERB ENDING IN "ING"

with us?

Gabriella

A NEW DUET

When Sharpay told me _____ would be
                        CELEBRITY (MALE)

having dinner with her and her family tonight, how could I

say _____? It was really _____ that she invited
     SILLY WORD   ADJECTIVE

me. It was a lot of _____. I can't believe
                    NOUN

that I might have a chance at playing _____ at
                                      TYPE OF SPORT

_____! I got so caught up in
PLACE

the moment I didn't even realize that I promised Sharpay I

would _____ onstage with her!
      VERB

LET'S PLAY BALL!

When I invited Ryan to _____ at
                                                    VERB

the staff softball game, I had no idea he'd be so

_____! When he stood on
                   ADJECTIVE

the _____'s mound and threw
                   OCCUPATION

the _____, you could tell that he
              NOUN

was totally going to help us _____ the
                                            VERB

game. He threw _____ strikes
                              NUMBER

in _____ innings. We were so excited
        NUMBER

we yelled _____ and _____ around
          SILLY WORD   VERB (PAST TENSE)

the field!

THINKING IT OVER

I've been so caught up in my new job as a/an

_____ and hanging out with
OCCUPATION

_____ that I _____ realized
CELEBRITY (MALE)   ADVERB

I haven't been spending that much time with Gabriella

or the rest of the _____. I think I'm going
NOUN

to ask _____ if I can have
PERSON IN ROOM (MALE)

my old job as a/an _____ back.
OCCUPATION

I'm going to _____ to all of my friends
VERB

and tell them how _____ I am. I hope
ADJECTIVE

they can forgive me.

THE BIG DAY

Today is the day of the talent show! I can't wait for Troy and

me to _____ together. It will be so _____.
        VERB   ADJECTIVE

My parents, _____, and
                    CELEBRITY (FEMALE)

_____ are going to be so excited!
        PERSON IN ROOM (MALE)

I hope they take lots of _____ of us. It has
                              PLURAL NOUN

always been my _____ to
                              NOUN

_____ onstage with Troy Bolton, and
        VERB

now it's finally coming true. _____!
                                    SILLY WORD

KEEPING PROMISES

I promised Sharpay that I would _____ with her at
VERB

the talent show, and I always keep my _____.
PLURAL NOUN

But it would be really _____ if the
ADJECTIVE

other _____ got to _____ with
PLURAL NOUN   VERB

us, too. I think when it's time to _____ I'm going
VERB

to tell Sharpay that we're all going to _____.
VERB

That is what the _____ spirit is
TYPE OF ANIMAL

all about!

TAKING THE STAGE

When Troy invited me and the rest of the _____ to
PLURAL NOUN

sing onstage I almost _____! We had such
VERB (PAST TENSE)

a blast, and I think the _____ really liked
PLURAL NOUN

us. Kelsi wrote a brand-new _____, and it was really
NOUN

_____. Everyone had such a great
ADJECTIVE

time _____ and _____.
VERB ENDING IN "ING"   VERB ENDING IN "ING"

Even Sharpay had a good _____. I'm so
NOUN

_____ that the _____ is back
ADJECTIVE   NOUN

together again!

TIME TO CELEBRATE!

The rest of the summer is going to be so _____!
ADJECTIVE

I'm going to keep my job as a/an _____ at
OCCUPATION

the _____ and spend as much time with
PLACE

my _____ as possible. After work, Gabriella
PLURAL NOUN

and I are going to do so many _____
ADJECTIVE

things. We'll go to the _____,
PLACE

play _____, and have _____
TYPE OF SPORT   ADJECTIVE

dinners. I'm really looking forward to my senior year

at _____, but until then, I'm going
SILLY WORD

to _____ and _____ as much as
VERB   VERB

possible. _____!
EXCLAMATION

A MAGICAL MUSICAL

This year's spring musical will be entitled *Senior Year*.

The enthusiasm displayed recently for theater

has been _____, and what

ADJECTIVE

better way to celebrate that than by immortalizing the

_____ seniors? Kelsi will, of course,

VERB ENDING IN "ING"

be composing the _____ for the show, while

NOUN

Ryan will display his amazing _____ abilities

VERB

in a solo performance. Troy will perform a modern version of

Romeo and _____, along with

PERSON IN THE ROOM (FEMALE)

Gabriella—another gifted _____.

OCCUPATION

Ms. DARBUS

LOOKING BACK ON EAST HIGH

In the past _____ years, East High
NUMBER

has taught me a great deal about myself and about

other _____, too. I mean, I never imagined
PLURAL NOUN

that a guy who likes to play _____ would
TYPE OF SPORT

love to _____ pastries! But it's possible to
VERB

break free from the status _____. Who
SILLY WORD

would've thought that I, Troy Bolton, the captain of

the _____ would be the lead
TYPE OF ANIMAL (PLURAL)

_____ in *Twinkle* _____! But most
OCCUPATION   NOUN

importantly, East High is what brought _____ and
CELEBRITY (FEMALE)

I together, and for that, I'm forever _____.
ADJECTIVE

TAKE A BOW

This is my last chance to be the _____ of an
NOUN

East High musical, and I'm not going to let Gabriella,

_____, or any of those
CELEBRITY (FEMALE)

other _____ Wildcats get in my way! I'll need
ADJECTIVE

to act _____. If I can devise a _____ to
ADVERB   NOUN

get Gabriella to _____ to attend the freshman
PLACE

honors program, then the duet with _____
PERSON IN THE ROOM (MALE)

will be mine!

CRAZY COMMITTEES

Honestly, I don't know what the big _____ is.
NOUN

The duties of the seniors are pretty _____ to
ADJECTIVE

follow. If they would all just _____ my agenda,
VERB

they'd be as organized as me!

- The Senior Trip Committee meets at _____
  PLACE

  every _____ morning.
  DAY OF THE WEEK

- The Prom Committee will be headed up by

  _____, and it convenes
  CELEBRITY (MALE)

  tomorrow and every other Tuesday henceforward.

  Pick up your tickets from _____
  PERSON IN THE ROOM (FEMALE)

  by this Friday.

- The final meeting of the _____ club
  SILLY WORD

  will be held next Tuesday.

  Taylor

TOTALLY TIARA

Tiara here—reporting for duty! As a sophomore, I know

how _____ it is to be the Queen Bee at school,
ADJECTIVE

like Sharpay _____ is, which is why I have
SILLY WORD

volunteered to be her _____. I've brought
OCCUPATION

her _____ when she's thirsty, done her
TYPE OF LIQUID

_____ assignments, and kept a calendar
LANGUAGE

of all of her social _____. I hope
PLURAL NOUN

all this hard _____ pays off. Maybe once
NOUN

Sharpay graduates, I'll be the new _____ at
NOUN

East High!

WELCOME TO THE WILDCATS!

Troy Bolton is, like, the coolest _____ at East High.
NOUN

I mean, he's the star of the _____ team,
TYPE OF SPORT

the _____ in the musicals, and he's got the coolest
NOUN

girlfriend—_____! He even passed
PERSON IN ROOM (FEMALE)

the _____ to me in the last few seconds of the big
NOUN

game so that I was the _____ who sunk
OCCUPATION

the winning _____. Now I'm known as Jimmy
NOUN

the _____. _____! Maybe Troy
NOUN   **EXCLAMATION**

will give me the locker he's had since _____,
YEAR

and I'll become as _____ as he is at
ADJECTIVE

East High!

COLLEGE APPLICATIONS 101

Getting accepted to college is no _____ task.
ADJECTIVE

Here are my winning _____ to make
PLURAL NOUN

your college _____ come true.
PLURAL NOUN

1. You'll _____ need to take
   ADVERB

   at least _____ Honors and
   NUMBER

   Advanced Placement classes.

2. Take a study course so you'll get a high _____ on
   NOUN

   your SAT's.

3. Participation in extracurricular activities such as playing

   _____ and joining the _____ club,
   TYPE OF SPORT   SILLY WORD

   shows that you are a well-rounded person.

U OF A—HERE I COME!

Wow, I am so _____ to _____ at
_{VERB (PAST TENSE)} _{VERB}

the University of Albuquerque in the fall! In just

_____ short months, I'll be heading there
_{NUMBER}

ready to _____ and play some b-ball.
_{VERB}

Troy and I will make a name for ourselves as the new

_____ who can handle the ball on the
_{PLURAL NOUN}

court just like our hero _____.
_{CELEBRITY (MALE)}

But even though I can't wait to be a member of

the _____ basketball team, I'll
_{SILLY WORD}

always be a Wildcat at heart!

JUILLIARD DREAMS

The Juilliard School is one of the world's premiere

_____ -arts conservatories. It has always been
VERB ENDING IN "ING"

a dream of mine to study _____ there.
SCHOOL SUBJECT

I could learn to compose _____ from the
PLURAL NOUN

finest _____ in the world. I really hope
OCCUPATION (PLURAL)

that I get in — they only accept _____ new students
NUMBER

per year. I'm going to keep my _____ crossed
PLURAL NOUN

and _____ for the best!
VERB

DRESSED TO IMPRESS

I am so excited that Kelsi agreed to _____ to the
_____(VERB)_____

prom with me. But I'm also a little bit _____.
_____(ADJECTIVE)_____

That's why I had Giorgio _____ himself
_____(SILLY WORD)_____

custom-design a _____ for me
_____(ARTICLE OF CLOTHING)_____

to wear. It's got a _____ lining with a matching
_____(COLOR)_____

vest and a/an _____ tie. Everything will match
_____(ADJECTIVE)_____

with Kelsi's prom _____. I think
_____(ARTICLE OF CLOTHING)_____

we're going to make a stunning _____.
_____(NOUN)_____

Maybe we'll even be voted Prom _____ and
_____(OCCUPATION)_____

_____!
_____(OCCUPATION)_____

LOCKER LOOT

Now that I'm leaving _____ it's time
                           PLACE

to pass my locker on to _____. Let's just
                          CELEBRITY (MALE)

say it's been a while—like about _____ years
                                    NUMBER

since I cleaned it out. First, I found my lucky pair of

_____, which haven't been
ARTICLE OF CLOTHING (PLURAL)

washed since _____. Maybe I'll pass
                   YEAR

those on to my locker's new owner as a good-luck _____.
                                                      NOUN

Then I found that _____ assignment
                        LANGUAGE

from sophomore year—I guess my _____ didn't
                                      ANIMAL

eat it after all. Finally, I unearthed the _____ Zeke
                                              TYPE OF FOOD

made for me last year. It leaked and formed a crust on the

bottom of the locker—_____!
                          EXCLAMATION

97

PROM-TACULAR!

My prom dress is _____! It is being flown in

from _____ and was custom-made for me
COUNTRY

by _____ . I had it modeled
PERSON IN THE ROOM (FEMALE)

after the one that _____ wore at
CELEBRITY (FEMALE)

the _____ Awards. The gown is _____ with
SILLY WORD   COLOR

delicate _____ on the neckline and hem.
PLURAL NOUN

And I found the most awesome _____ to
PLURAL NOUN

match! They are _____ and have
COLOR

a _____ inch heel. And, of course, I borrowed my
NUMBER

jewelry from jeweler-to-the-stars, _____ .
PERSON IN ROOM (MALE)

How fabulous is that!

DANCING 101

No matter if you are hitting the dance floor for the first time

or if you are a seasoned _____, these
                            OCCUPATION

tips will make you look _____!
                        ADJECTIVE

1. _____ is all about confidence.
   VERB ENDING IN "ING"

   Hold your _____ high and smile.
              NOUN

2. Watch some music videos to pick up some _____ moves.
                                            ADJECTIVE

3. Lose yourself in the sound of the _____.
                                     NOUN

   Let your _____ move _____
            NOUN   ADVERB

   to the beats and rhythms.

BREAKTHROUGH

I have to hand it to her. Ever since that girl

_____ showed up at East
PERSON IN ROOM (FEMALE)

High and shook up the status quo, my life has been

_____. I mean, before that, I had to bake
ADJECTIVE

in secret, worried that _____ would
CELEBRITY (FEMALE)

find out and _____ all over school. But now, I can
VERB

hold my _____ high and declare that I, Zeke Baylor,
NOUN

love to make _____, especially when
TYPE OF FOOD (PLURAL)

they're topped with _____. (I definitely
PLURAL NOUN

like to bake for Sharpay—she recognizes my skills!)

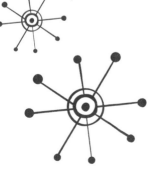

TROY'S CHOICE

It's been a dream of mine to be the star _____ for
_{OCCUPATION}

the University of Albuquerque _____ since
_{SILLY WORD}

I was a little _____. But now that I've discovered
_{NOUN}

that I also love to _____, I'm not sure that
_{VERB}

playing _____ is what I'm all about. I mean,
_{TYPE OF SPORT}

this Juilliard thing really threw me for a _____,
_{NOUN}

that's for sure. I feel like I'll be letting Chad and my father

down if I don't _____ U of A. But won't I be
_{VERB}

letting myself down if I don't at least think about a future as a

possible _____? Maybe I can find a school that
_{OCCUPATION}

will allow me to be Troy Bolton, basketball _____, and
_{NOUN}

Troy Bolton, performer. . . .

GABRIELLA'S CHOICE

_____! I can't believe it. I got my letter

EXCLAMATION

from _____ today and have been accepted into

PLACE

their freshman honors _____.

NOUN

I am so _____ that my _____ are

ADJECTIVE ... PLURAL NOUN

shaking. I've worked so hard for this! So, why do I feel

so _____? It's just that I've never had

ADJECTIVE

a place that really felt like home before. I have made

so many incredible _____ at East High.

PLURAL NOUN

So, how am I supposed to just pick up and _____ away

VERB

from all of that? Maybe Stanford can _____ for

VERB

another year. . . .

MY ESCAPE

Have you ever felt like there was only one place in the

_____ that is truly your _____?

NOUN   NOUN

Well, for me, that place is my tree house. My father and I

built it in _____, when I was just _____

YEAR   NUMBER

years old. And the only _____ I've

NOUN

ever let come into my treehouse is my mom—until

I let _____, that is. Being up in my

CELEBRITY (FEMALE)

tree house gives me a/an _____ perspective on

ADJECTIVE

life, my future, and especially my _____—the truly

NOUN

important things in life. _____ up there

VERB ENDING IN "ING"

makes me feel as if no matter what decisions I make, they'll

be the right ones.

SURPRISE DATE

I'm not really sure what just happened, but apparently, I'm

taking Sharpay to the _____! I
                          PLACE

approached her in the _____, even though
                          ROOM

I was so _____. Luckily my friend
              ADJECTIVE

Jason _____ was there
          LAST NAME OF PERSON IN ROOM

to _____ me beforehand. But before I could
      VERB

say _____, Sharpay was telling me that
        SILLY WORD

we would be _____ together! She is
              VERB ENDING IN "ING"

getting her prom _____ flown in
                    TYPE OF CLOTHING

from _____, and she wants me to take
        COUNTRY

dance _____. _____ !
        PLURAL NOUN   EXCLAMATION

ZEKE

PROM PRIMPING

1. Schedule an appointment for a facial at least two weeks

   before the prom so your _____ will really

   NOUN

   look _____.

   ADJECTIVE

2. Ask _____ to trim _____ inches off

   PERSON IN THE ROOM (FEMALE)   NUMBER

   your hair so it will look healthy and _____.

   ADJECTIVE

3. The day before the prom, make sure to _____ to

   VERB

   the _____ salon for a mani and pedi.

   NOUN

4. Use _____ -whitening strips on your _____

   SILLY WORD   PLURAL NOUN

   for a _____ -dollar smile.

   NUMBER

DANCING IN THE DARK

I almost _____ when I walked out
VERB (PAST TENSE)

of _____ class and spotted Troy—here at
NOUN

Stanford! He was sitting in the _____ and was wearing
PLACE

a fancy _____! It was the most _____ thing
TYPE OF CLOTHING   ADJECTIVE

anyone has ever done for me. Of course, I graciously accepted

his offer for a _____. We got so swept away in
VERB

the moment that it was almost like being at the prom at East

High. I think I'm learning that while home may be where

the _____ is, my heart is wherever Troy is.
NOUN

FINALS CRUNCH

_____ for final exams is always a

VERB ENDING IN "ING"

difficult task, but the gang from East High knows just how to

make _____ easier!

VERB ENDING IN "ING"

1. Before finals are in full swing, schedule time to _____
   VERB

   at least _____ hours every night.
   NUMBER

2. Schedule a study break at least every hour or so. Drink

   a cup of _____, or go for a
   TYPE OF LIQUID

   walk around the _____.
   NOUN

3. Pick a/an _____ and comfortable
   ADJECTIVE

   place to study. It should be well-lit, quiet, and free of

   distractions, such as blaring _____.
   PLURAL NOUN

WILDCATS' LAST YEAR

It's finally coming to an end. Troy, Chad, Jason, and the

other _____ are _____, and I'll
    TYPE OF ANIMAL (PLURAL)   VERB ENDING IN "ING"

have to work with a new crop of basketball _____.
                                              PLURAL NOUN

I'll really feel _____ next year when I can't walk onto
               ADVERB

the court and see all of my favorite _____ every day.
                                       PLURAL NOUN

But there are some promising new _____ that
                                  OCCUPATION (PLURAL)

I think really have the Wildcat spirit, especially Jimmie Zara.

The basket he _____ in the final
               VERB (PAST TENSE)

game was _____, so maybe we can keep
          ADJECTIVE

our winning streak alive. _____ Wildcats!
                           VERB

Coach Bolton

108

HEADED TO JUILLIARD

Of the _____ applicants to Juilliard, not only was
NUMBER

I accepted, but I was awarded a _____ (along with
NOUN

Ryan—a true talent.) All of my Juilliard _____ are
PLURAL NOUN

about to come true, and I could not feel more _____!
ADJECTIVE

Just picture me sitting by a _____ in the hallowed
NOUN

halls of Juilliard, singing and _____ with
VERB ENDING IN "ING"

people like _____. And I get
PERSON IN ROOM (FEMALE)

to do it in the Big _____: New York City!
TYPE OF FOOD

Wish me luck!

FAREWELL, EAST HIGH

I've had plenty of practice saying _____ in the
                                    EXCLAMATION

past, but this time is different. This time, I've been able to stay

at the same school for a while, and _____ isn't
                                     VERB ENDING IN "ING"

going to be easy. The musicals, the Scholastic Decathlons,

the _____ rallies and _____ games . . .
      SILLY WORD   NOUN

And, of course, the _____ here at
                        PLURAL NOUN

East High have meant so much to me. I only hope that when I'm

a new _____ once again at Stanford,
          OCCUPATION

I'll feel as _____ as I did when I was
                ADJECTIVE

a new _____ at East High.
          NOUN

FOLLOW YOUR DREAMS

_____! I can't believe I actually told my

EXCLAMATION

_____ and my best friend, _____, that

NOUN   **CELEBRITY (MALE)**

I wanted to _____ at _____ instead

VERB   **PLACE**

of U of A. I'm really glad that I made that decision. They have

a/an _____ theater program *and* a/an

ADJECTIVE

_____ _____ team.

ADJECTIVE   **TYPE OF SPORT**

And I'll only be _____ miles away from

NUMBER

_____ at Stanford. I can't wait to see

PERSON IN ROOM (FEMALE)

what the future has in store for me. Farewell, Wildcats!